To Jennifer, for being an amazing sister,
and to our parents for having us
hold hands when we argued
—J.R.

To my brother, Matt, who made drinking milk
at dinner a race, and to our parents for letting us scream
"MILKED YA!" for the win
—L.R.

Library of Congress Control Number: 2015952476
ISBN 978-0-06-240359-9

The artist used polymer clay, pastels, acrylic paint, wire, and a macro lens
to create the illustrations for this book.
Typography by Erin Fitzsimmons
16 17 18 19 20 SCP 10 9 8 7 6 5 4 3 2 1

First Edition

Sweet Competition

By
Liz and
Jimmy
Reed

HARPER
An Imprint of HarperCollins*Publishers*

The cherry twins were always trying
to outdo each other.

Everything was a competition.

Everything.

Today's Flavors

 strawberry   vanilla   chocolate   the 'bow

One
small scoop
to share,
please.

SIZES

SMALL
TASTE

DOUBLE
SCOOP

MEGA
CONE

When they saw a chance to prove who was *really* the best,

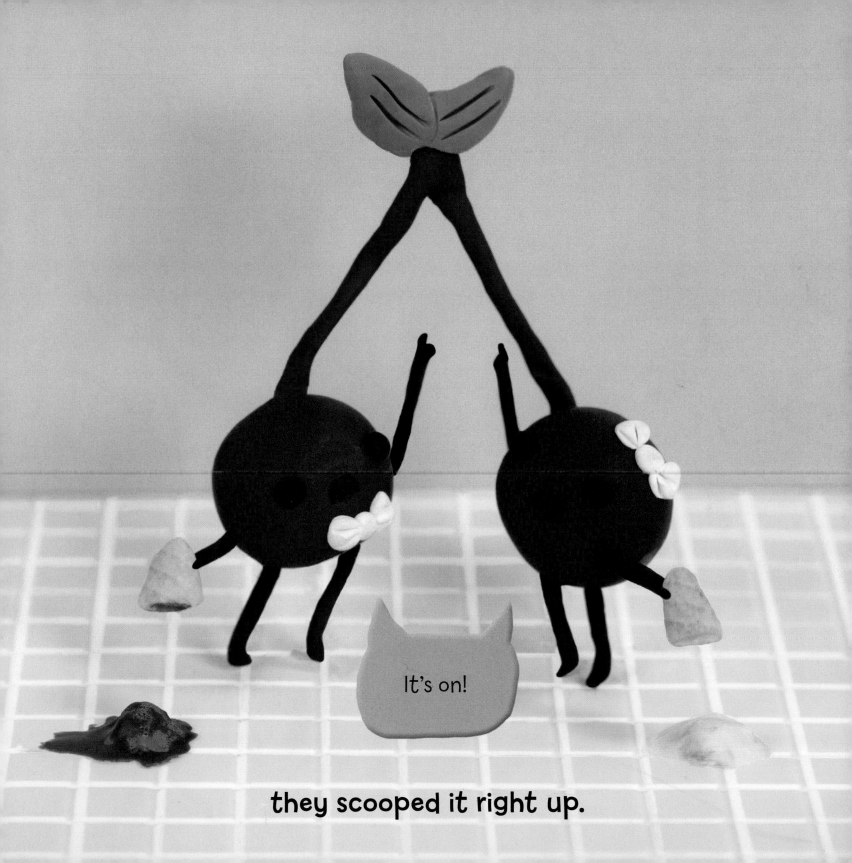

they scooped it right up.

They formed two separate teams.

Then the cherries remembered one minor detail.
They were connected.

Since they were just practicing, the teams agreed that the cherries could stay together. For now.

BANANA'S
SKY HIGH SPLIT
12 Cherries High!

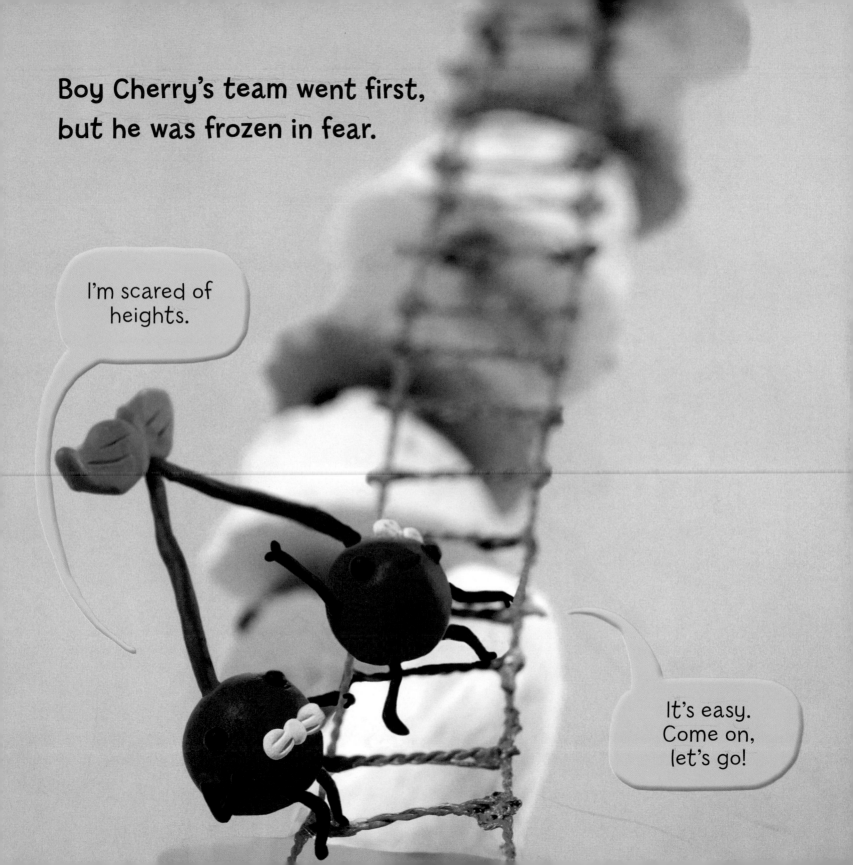

and savored the view.

Girl Cherry went next,

but the pit in her stomach knew something was up.

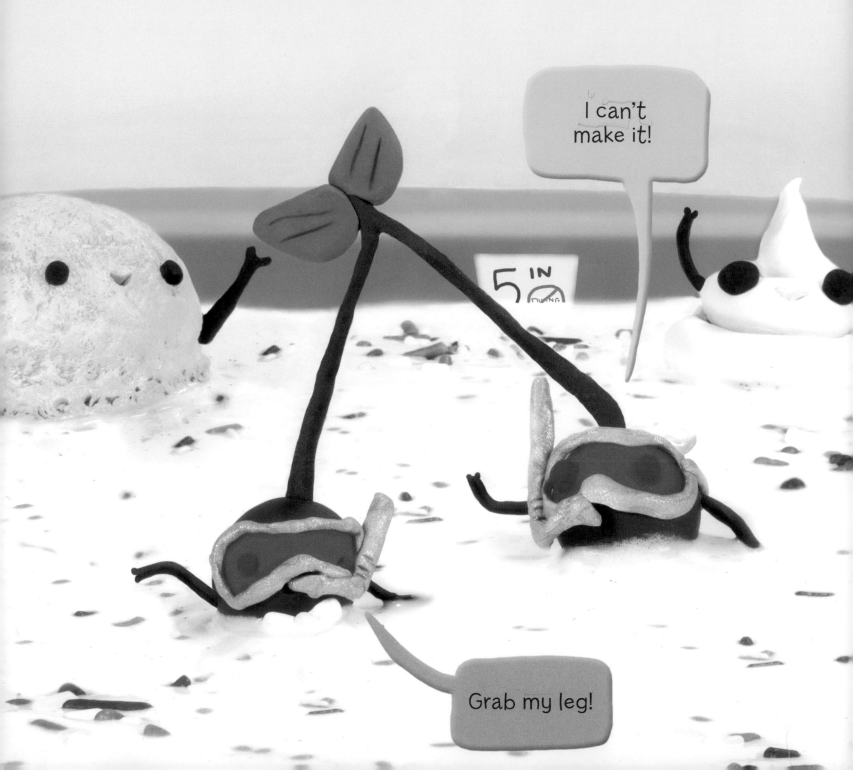

and made it safely to Brownie's float.

Working as a team wasn't so bad.

But their teamwork didn't last long.

The cherries knew what had to be done.

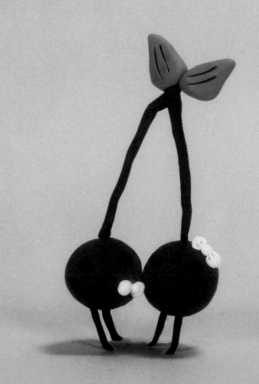

Instead of separating, they cooked up a plan.

Once they got to the contest,

CAKE SUNDAE

No Ice Cream Sundae

the competition was thick (and creamy)!

ICE CREAM SAMMY SUNDAE

CELERY ICE CREAM SUNDAE

At the big event, the cherries
were on top of everything.

Working together, they were victorious.

DOUBLE CHERRY

SPLIT

13 CHERRIES
Wide

As a team,
they beat two smart cookies
and even took the cake.

The trophy was theirs . . .

to share.

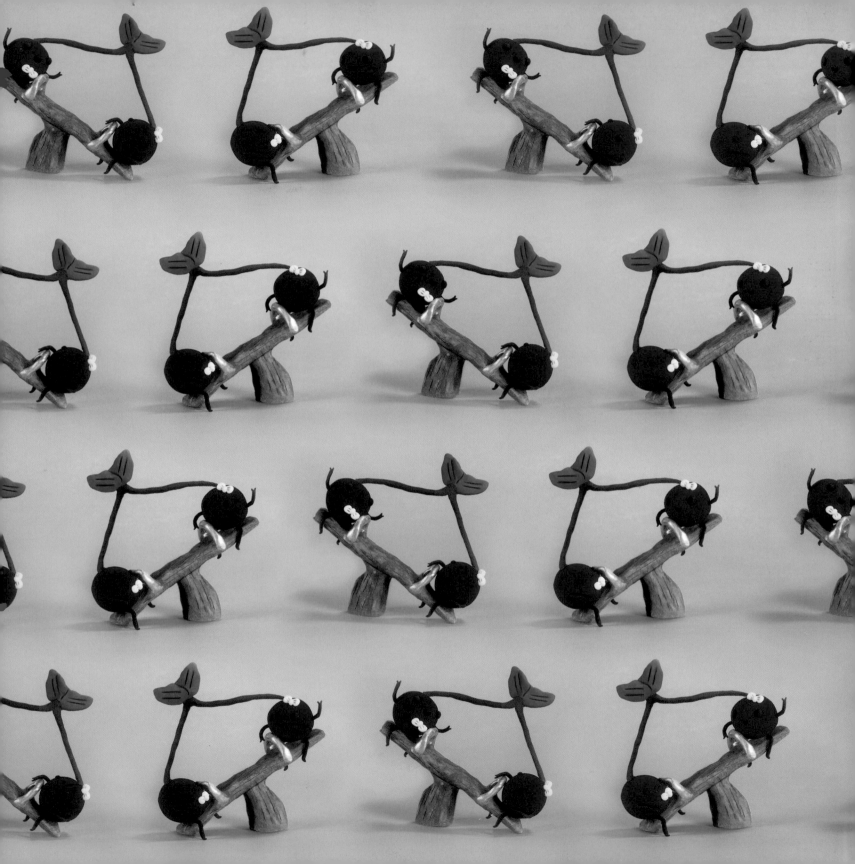